The Rime of the Ancient Mariner

The Rime of the Ancient Mariner

SAMUEL TAYLOR COLERIDGE
WITH THE CLASSIC ILLUSTRATIONS BY
GUSTAVE DORÉ

CHARTWELL
BOOKS, INC.

This edition printed in 2008 by
CHARTWELL BOOKS, INC.
A Division of **BOOK SALES, INC.**
114 Northfield Avenue
Edison, New Jersey 08837

Copyright © 2008 Arcturus Publishing Limited
26/27 Bickels Yard, 151–153 Bermondsey Street,
London SE1 3HA

ISBN-13: 978-0-7858-2340-7
ISBN-10: 0-7858-2340-9

Printed in China

CONTENTS

INTRODUCTION

Although 'The Rime of the Ancient Mariner' is now widely acclaimed as one of the best narrative poems in English, contemporary critics were underwhelmed when it appeared in 1798. The 'Ancient Mariner' was published anonymously in the *Lyrical Ballads*, a collection of poems by Samuel Taylor Coleridge and William Wordsworth. The volume sold slowly, and it was reported that many copies were sold to sailors who were disgruntled to find that it did not contain the collection of sea shanties they were hoping for. But *Lyrical Ballads* is now seen as a turning point in the history of English poetry. It marked the beginning of the Romantic movement in England, which advocated the use of everyday language and favoured emotion, nature and the imagination as fit subjects for poetry.

'The Rime of the Ancient Mariner' relates a supernatural adventure with a spiritual resolution. After committing a crime against Nature, the Mariner endures a terrible, solitary experience until his soul is awakened to the splendour of the natural world and his kinship with it. The individual confronting the wonder of Nature and finding fulfilment in its embrace it is a central motif of Romantic poetry, and nowhere better exemplified than in the figure of the Mariner.

Gustave Doré's powerful and beautiful illustrations, presented here with the poem, brilliantly evoke the terrible majesty of nature and the Mariner's humanity.

COLERIDGE'S LIFE

Samuel Taylor Coleridge was born on 21 October 1772 in the village of Ottery St Mary, Devon. In 1781 his father died and Coleridge was sent to the school of Christ's Hospital in London. The abrupt end to his rural boyhood pained him and he mourns its loss in 'Frost at Midnight' (p. 96). Coleridge was something of a child prodigy; he read widely and learned foreign languages with ease. As an adult, he could read in German, Italian, Latin, Greek, Spanish, French and Portuguese.

In 1791 Coleridge went to Jesus College, Cambridge. He quickly ran out of money and in 1793 enlisted as a dragoon, using the unlikely assumed name of Silas Tomkyn Comberbache. But Coleridge was not cavalryman material. He couldn't ride – he didn't even like horses – and he was so bad at grooming and cleaning the tack that his horse was a disgrace to the army. Eventually, his brothers secured his release and he returned to Cambridge in 1794. Even so, he never finished his degree.

Coleridge's imagination was fired by the social and philosophical issues stirred up by the French Revolution. A chance meeting with the poet Robert Southey led him to seek a utopian solution to social injustice, and the pair formulated a plan to set up a community in Pennsylvania where children would be brought up and educated according to the philosophy of Rousseau and Voltaire. The plan never came to anything and their youthful idealism ended bitterly. Southey married his fiancé Edith Fricker and ran away to Portugal with her – but not before persuading Coleridge to marry Edith's sister Sarah. It was a match as ill-fated as it was ill-conceived.

In 1797 Coleridge embarked upon the relationship with William Wordsworth and his sister, Dorothy, which would be central to his life as a poet. Dorothy kept diaries which have given us a valuable insight into their complex relationship; Coleridge described them as 'three people, but only one soul'. In July 1797, the Wordsworths moved to an old mansion close to Coleridge's home in Nether Stowey, Somerset. This was the happiest and most successful year of Coleridge's life; he wrote 'The Rime of the Ancient Mariner', the first part of the long poem 'Christabel' and the fragment 'Kubla Khan' amongst others. But all was not well. By this time Coleridge was taking opium, at first medicinally. He seems to have slipped quite quickly into addiction and became increasingly dependent on the drug over the years.

Coleridge and Wordsworth went to Germany in the autumn of 1798 and were away for nearly a year, so they were absent when *Lyrical Ballads* was published in England. They were also away when Coleridge's second child died, still a baby. This tragedy did not precipitate Coleridge's return home, and when he eventually did, his relationship with his wife deteriorated rapidly.

Wordsworth married his childhood friend Mary Hutchinson, and Coleridge promptly fell in love with her sister, also called Sarah. Although it was never consummated, Coleridge was caused much anguish by this new passion. 'Dejection: An Ode' (p. 102), written in 1802, expresses the despair brought on by his fruitless love, his failing marriage, his increasing dependency on opium and his philosophical and spiritual struggles. Although Coleridge and Sarah Fricker went on to have two further children, the couple eventually separated. Sarah Hutchinson lived with the Wordsworth trio for many years and never married.

Coleridge, usually penniless, drifted around England and Europe, staying with various friends and borrowing money from them, taking paid work intermittently – he even worked as a Private Secretary and spy in Malta in 1804. He had hoped that his time in Europe would help to improve his health, but he was disappointed. However, he determined to be resolute on his return to England, separating from his wife in 1806. When Sarah Hutchinson eventually moved to Wales in 1810, finding the strain of her relationship with Coleridge too much to bear, Coleridge also broke with Wordsworth whom he believed had encouraged her to leave.

Coleridge became increasingly interested in and preoccupied with German philosophy and less committed to poetry, writing in a variety of other genres. In 1817 he wrote *Biographia Literaria*, a long and complex combination of autobiography, literary criticism and thought on literary theory, which has become a key text in the history of literary criticism in England.

He spent the last 18 years of his life, from 1816, living in the home of his doctor and friend, Dr James Gillman, in London. Here Gillman regulated Coleridge's doses of opium and tried to calm him when he was terrorized by the nightmares his addiction produced. Coleridge died in 1834.

THE RIME OF THE ANCIENT MARINER

A neighbour, John Cruikshank, described to Coleridge a dream which intrigued the poet; it featured 'a skeleton ship, with figures in it'. On a walk through the Quantock Hills, in Somerset, on 13 November 1797, Coleridge discussed his ideas for a new poem with William and Dorothy Wordsworth. Years later, Wordsworth recalled:

'In the course of this walk was planned the poem of the "Ancient Mariner"... Much the greatest part of the story was Mr Coleridge's invention, but certain parts I suggested; for example, some crime was to be committed which should bring upon the Old Navigator, as Coleridge afterwards delighted to call him, the spectral persecution, as a consequence of that crime and his own wanderings. I had been reading in Shelvocke's Voyages *a day or two before, that while doubling Cape Horn, they frequently saw albatrosses in that latitude, the largest sort of sea fowl, some extending their wings twelve or thirteen feet. "Suppose," said I, "you represent him as having killed one of these*

birds on entering the South Sea, and the tutelary spirits of these regions take upon them to avenge the crime." The incident was thought fit for the purpose, and adopted accordingly. I also suggested the navigation of the ship by the dead men, but do not recollect that I had anything more to do with the scheme of the poem.'

Coleridge worked on the poem for four months, then read it to Dorothy and William on 23 March 1798. It was nothing like anything he had written before and is widely considered his best poem.

GUSTAVE DORÉ'S ILLUSTRATIONS

Paul Gustave Doré was born in Strasbourg, France on 6 January 1832, two years before Coleridge's death. He, too, was a child prodigy, with his earliest dated drawings produced at the age of five. By the age of 12, Doré was carving lithographic stones and printing illustrations to stories. Over the course of his life he would produce more than 10,000 pictures. Although he was also a painter and sculptor, it is for his woodcuts and engravings that he is most famous.

Doré's introduction to paid work was dramatic. At the age of 15 he visited Paris with his parents, and noticed some engravings in the window display of a publisher. The next morning, he pretended to be ill and, when his parents went out, he produced some sketches illustrating the same subjects as the pictures he had seen and took them to the publisher. The publisher, Charles Philipon, was astonished and asked him to do more – which Doré accomplished in minutes. Philipon refused to let Doré leave the shop, had his father tracked down and negotiated a contract with him on the spot. When the family returned to Strasbourg, Doré remained behind and moved in with Philipon. Within a year, he was the toast of Paris and the most highly paid illustrator in the country.

Doré began working with English publishers in 1853, starting with a commission to illustrate the poems of Lord Byron (another Romantic poet inspired by Coleridge and Wordsworth). He spent three months a year in London for five years working on 180 engravings for *London: A Portrait* published in 1872. This was criticized at the time for concentrating on images of poverty, but has been acclaimed ever since for the quality of the work.

Doré's illustrations for the 'Rime of the Ancient Mariner' were published in 1876. His sympathy for the human condition, combined with his interest in supernatural subjects, made the 'Ancient Mariner' an ideal vehicle for his talent. The eerie, fog-drenched scenes made the most of his personal style. The collection continued a trend for Gothic horror begun with his ambitious illustrations for Dante's *Divine Comedy* and culminating in his illustrations for Edgar Allan Poe's 'The Raven'. Poe was the writer and Doré the illustrator who would set the standards for literary horror. 'The Raven' was Doré's last published work; he died in 1882, at the age of 51.

STEEL ENGRAVINGS

Doré's illustrations for 'Ancient Mariner' are engravings, produced by cutting the image into a steel plate with a special tool called a burin. Ink is wiped over the engraved plate, filling the grooves. Surplus ink is cleaned away and the plate pressed against paper to transfer the image. The engraved plate is always a mirror image of the final illustration.

OTHER POEMS

The selection of other poems by Coleridge represents some of his best and most characteristically 'romantic' poems. 'Frost at Midnight' and 'This Lime-Tree Bower' are so-called conversation poems. This is a form pioneered by Coleridge and adopted by Wordsworth. It has come to be the principal model of much modern poetry.

'Kubla Khan' was, according to Coleridge, inspired by a dream (possibly fuelled by opium), that was interrupted by a visitor he refers to as a 'person from Porlock'. Coleridge was never able to recall the rest of the dream and finish the poem.

All the poems are taken from the 1834 edition by William Pickering.

Most of the images decorating this chapter are from engravings by Thomas Bewick (1753–1828) and his school. Bewick was an artist and engraver of some note, and was particularly renowned for his books on ornithology, the *History of Birds*, produced 1797–1804.

The Rime of the Ancient Mariner

IN SEVEN PARTS

PART THE FIRST

An ancient Mariner
meeteth three gallants
bidden to a wedding
feast, and detaineth
one.

IT is an ancient Mariner,
And he stoppeth one of three.
'By thy long grey beard and glittering eye,
Now wherefore stopp'st thou me?

'The Bridegroom's doors are opened wide,
And I am next of kin;
The guests are met, the feast is set:
May'st hear the merry din.'

He holds him with his skinny hand,
'There was a ship,' quoth he.
'Hold off! unhand me, grey-beard loon!'
Eftsoons his hand dropt he.

The Wedding-Guest is
spell-bound by the eye
of the old seafaring
man, and constrained
to hear his tale.

He holds him with his glittering eye –
The Wedding-Guest stood still,
And listens like a three years' child:
The Mariner hath his will.

'By thy long grey beard and glittering eye, / Now wherefore stopp'st thou me?

The Wedding-Guest sat on a stone:
He cannot choose but hear;
And thus spake on that ancient man,
The bright-eyed Mariner.

The Mariner tells how
the ship sailed
southward with a good
wind and fair weather,
till it reached the Line.

The ship was cheered, the harbour cleared,
Merrily did we drop
Below the kirk, below the hill,
Below the light-house top.

The Sun came up upon the left,
Out of the sea came he!
And he shone bright, and on the right
Went down into the sea.

The Wedding-Guest sat on a stone: / He cannot choose but hear;

Higher and higher every day,
Till over the mast at noon –
The Wedding-Guest here beat his breast,
For he heard the loud bassoon.

The Wedding-Guest
heareth the bridal
music; but the Mariner
continueth his tale.

The bride hath paced into the hall,
Red as a rose is she;
Nodding their heads before her goes
The merry minstrelsy.

The Wedding-Guest he beat his breast,
Yet he cannot choose but hear;
And thus spake on that ancient man,
The bright-eyed Mariner.

The bride hath paced into the hall, / Red as a rose is she;

The ship drawn by a
storm toward the
South Pole.

And now the STORM-BLAST came, and he
Was tyrannous and strong:
He struck with his o'ertaking wings,
And chased us south along.

With sloping masts and dipping prow,
As who pursued with yell and blow
Still treads the shadow of his foe
And forward bends his head,
The ship drove fast, loud roared the blast,
And southward aye we fled.

And now the STORM-BLAST came, and he / Was tyrannous and strong:

And now there came both mist and snow,
And it grew wondrous cold:
And ice, mast-high, came floating by,
As green as emerald.

And now there came both mist and snow, / And it grew wondrous cold:

The land of ice, and of fearful sounds, where no living thing was to be seen.

And through the drifts the snowy clifts
Did send a dismal sheen:
Nor shapes of men nor beasts we ken –
The ice was all between.

The ice was here, the ice was there,
The ice was all around:
It cracked and growled, and roared and howled,
Like noises in a swound!

Till a great sea-bird, called the Albatross, came through the snow-fog, and was received with great joy and hospitality.

At length did cross an Albatross:
Thorough the fog it came;
As if it had been a Christian soul,
We hailed it in God's name.

The ice was here, the ice was there, / The ice was all around:

And lo! the Albatross
proveth a bird of good
omen, and followeth
the ship as it returned
northward through fog
and floating ice.

It ate the food it ne'er had eat,
And round and round it flew.
The ice did split with a thunder-fit;
The helmsman steered us through!

And a good south wind sprung up behind;
The Albatross did follow,
And every day, for food or play,
Came to the mariners' hollo!

In mist or cloud, on mast or shroud,
It perched for vespers nine;
Whiles all the night, through fog-smoke white,
Glimmered the white Moon-shine.

And every day, for food or play, / Came to the mariners' hollo!

The ancient Mariner
inhospitably killeth the
pious bird of good
omen.

'God save thee, ancient Mariner!
From the fiends, that plague thee thus! –
Why look'st thou so?' – With my cross-bow
I shot the ALBATROSS.

With my cross-bow / I shot the ALBATROSS.

PART THE SECOND

His shipmates cry out
against the ancient
Mariner, for killing the
bird of good luck.

THE Sun now rose upon the right:
Out of the sea came he,
Still hid in mist, and on the left
Went down into the sea.

And the good south wind still blew behind
But no sweet bird did follow,
Nor any day for food or play
Came to the mariners' hollo!

And I had done a hellish thing,
And it would work 'em woe:
For all averred, I had killed the bird
That made the breeze to blow.
Ah wretch! said they, the bird to slay
That made the breeze to blow!

And I had done a hellish thing, / And it would work 'em woe:

But when the fog cleared off, they justify the same, and thus make themselves accomplices in the crime.

Nor dim nor red, like God's own head,
The glorious Sun uprist:
Then all averred, I had killed the bird
That brought the fog and mist.
'Twas right, said they, such birds to slay,
That bring the fog and mist.

The fair breeze continues; the ship enters the Pacific Ocean, and sails northward, even till it reaches the Line.

The fair breeze blew, the white foam flew,
The furrow followed free:
We were the first that ever burst
Into that silent sea.

The ship hath been suddenly becalmed.

Down dropt the breeze, the sails dropt down,
'Twas sad as sad could be;
And we did speak only to break
The silence of the sea!

All in a hot and copper sky,
The bloody Sun, at noon,
Right up above the mast did stand,
No bigger than the Moon.

Day after day, day after day,
We stuck, nor breath nor motion;
As idle as a painted ship
Upon a painted ocean.

Day after day, day after day, / We stuck, nor breath nor motion;

And the Albatross
begins to be avenged.

Water, water, every where,
And all the boards did shrink;
Water, water, every where,
Nor any drop to drink.

The very deep did rot: O Christ!
That ever this should be!
Yea, slimy things did crawl with legs
Upon the slimy sea.

About, about, in reel and rout
The death-fires danced at night;
The water, like a witch's oils,
Burnt green, and blue and white.

About, about, in reel and rout / The death-fires danced at night;

A Spirit had followed them; one of the invisible inhabitants of this planet, neither departed souls nor angels; concerning whom the learned Jew, Josephus, and the Platonic Constantinopolitan, Michael Psellus, may be consulted. They are very numerous, and there is no climate or element without one or more. The shipmates in their sore distress, would fain throw the whole guilt on the ancient Mariner: in sign whereof they hang the dead sea-bird round his neck.

And some in dreams assuréd were
Of the Spirit that plagued us so:
Nine fathom deep he had followed us
From the land of mist and snow.

And every tongue, through utter drought,
Was withered at the root;
We could not speak, no more than if
We had been choked with soot.

Ah! well-a-day! what evil looks
Had I from old and young!
Instead of the cross, the Albatross
About my neck was hung.

Nine fathom deep he had followed us / From the land of mist and snow.

PART THE THIRD

The ancient Mariner
beholdeth a sign in the
element afar off.

THERE passed a weary time. Each throat
Was parched, and glazed each eye.
A weary time! a weary time!
How glazed each weary eye,
When looking westward, I beheld
A something in the sky.

At first it seemed a little speck,
And then it seemed a mist:
It moved and moved, and took at last
A certain shape, I wist.

A speck, a mist, a shape, I wist!
And still it neared and neared:
As if it dodged a water-sprite,
It plunged and tacked and veered.

At its nearer approach,
it seemeth him to be a
ship; and at a dear
ransom he freeth his
speech from the bonds
of thirst.

With throats unslaked, with black lips baked,
We could not laugh nor wail;
Through utter drought all dumb we stood!
I bit my arm, I sucked the blood,
And cried, A sail! a sail!

With throats unslaked, with black lips baked,
Agape they heard me call:

A flash of joy;

Gramercy! they for joy did grin,
And all at once their breath drew in,
As they were drinking all.

When looking westward, I beheld / A something in the sky.

And horror follows. For can it be a ship that comes onward without wind or tide?

See! see! (I cried) she tacks no more!
Hither to work us weal;
Without a breeze, without a tide,
She steadies with upright keel!

The western wave was all a-flame
The day was well nigh done!
Almost upon the western wave
Rested the broad bright Sun;
When that strange shape drove suddenly
Betwixt us and the Sun.

It seemeth him but the skeleton of a ship.

And straight the Sun was flecked with bars,
(Heaven's Mother send us grace!),
As if through a dungeon-grate he peered,
With broad and burning face.

Alas! (thought I, and my heart beat loud)
How fast she nears and nears!
Are those her sails that glance in the Sun,
Like restless gossameres!

And its ribs are seen as bars on the face of the setting Sun. The Spectre-Woman and her Death-mate, and no other on board the skeleton ship.

Are those her ribs through which the Sun
Did peer, as through a grate?
And is that Woman all her crew?
Is that a DEATH? and are there two?
Is DEATH that woman's mate?

And is that Woman all her crew? / Is that a DEATH?

Like vessel, like crew!

Her lips were red, her looks were free,
Her locks were yellow as gold:
Her skin was as white as leprosy,
The Night-Mare LIFE-IN-DEATH was she,
Who thicks man's blood with cold.

Death and Life-in-
Death have diced for
the ship's crew, and
she (the latter)
winneth the ancient
Mariner.

The naked hulk alongside came,
And the twain were casting dice;
'The game is done! I've won! I've won!'
Quoth she, and whistles thrice.

No twilight within the
courts of the Sun.

The Sun's rim dips; the stars rush out:
At one stride comes the dark;
With far-heard whisper, o'er the sea,
Off shot the spectre-bark.

We listened and looked sideways up!
Fear at my heart, as at a cup,
My life-blood seemed to sip!
The stars were dim, and thick the night,

At the rising of the
Moon,

The steersman's face by his lamp gleamed white;
From the sails the dew did drip –
Till clomb above the eastern bar
The hornéd Moon, with one bright star
Within the nether tip.

One after one, by the star-dogged Moon
Too quick for groan or sigh,

One after another,

Each turned his face with a ghastly pang,
And cursed me with his eye.

Each turned his face with a ghastly pang, / And cursed me with his eye.

His shipmates drop
down dead;

Four times fifty living men,
(And I heard nor sigh nor groan)
With heavy thump, a lifeless lump,
They dropped down one by one.

The souls did from their bodies fly, –
But Life-in-Death
They fled to bliss or woe!
begins her work on the
And every soul, it passed me by,
ancient Mariner.
Like the whizz of my CROSS-BOW!

And every soul, it passed me by, / Like the whizz of my CROSS-BOW!

PART THE FOURTH

The Wedding-Guest
feareth that a spirit is
talking to him;

'I FEAR thee, ancient Mariner!
I fear thy skinny hand!
And thou art long, and lank, and brown,
As is the ribbed sea-sand.

'I fear thee and thy glittering eye,
And thy skinny hand, so brown.' –

But the ancient
Mariner assureth him
of his bodily life, and
proceedeth to relate
his horrible penance.

Fear not, fear not, thou Wedding-Guest!
This body dropt not down.

Alone, alone, all, all alone,
Alone on a wide wide sea!
And never a saint took pity on
My soul in agony.

The many men, so beautiful!
And they all dead did lie:

He despiseth the
creatures of the calm,

And a thousand thousand slimy things
Lived on; and so did I.

I looked upon the rotting sea,
And drew my eyes away;

And envieth that they
should live, and so
many lie dead.

I looked upon the rotting deck,
And there the dead men lay.

I looked upon the rotting sea, / And drew my eyes away;

I looked to Heaven, and tried to pray:
But or ever a prayer had gusht,
A wicked whisper came, and made
My heart as dry as dust.

I closed my lids, and kept them close,
And the balls like pulses beat;
For the sky and the sea, and the sea and the sky,
Lay like a load on my weary eye,
And the dead were at my feet.

But the curse liveth for
him in the eye of the
dead men.

The cold sweat melted from their limbs,
Nor rot nor reek did they:
The look with which they looked on me
Had never passed away.

And the dead were at my feet.

An orphan's curse would drag to Hell
A spirit from on high;
But oh! more horrible than that
Is a curse in a dead man's eye!
Seven days, seven nights, I saw that curse,
And yet I could not die.

In his loneliness and fixedness he yearneth towards the journeying Moon, and the stars that still sojourn, yet still move onward; and everywhere the blue sky belongs to them, and is their appointed rest and their native country and their own natural homes, which they enter unannounced, as lords that are certainly expected, and yet there is a silent joy at their arrival.

The moving Moon went up the sky,
And no where did abide:
Softly she was going up,
And a star or two beside.

Her beams bemocked the sultry main,
Like April hoar-frost spread;
But where the ship's huge shadow lay,
The charmèd water burnt alway
A still and awful red.

Her beams bemocked the sultry main, / Like April hoar-frost spread;

By the light of the
Moon he beholdeth
God's creatures of the
great calm.

Beyond the shadow of the ship,
I watched the water-snakes:
They moved in tracks of shining white,
And when they reared, the elfish light
Fell off in hoary flakes.

Within the shadow of the ship
I watched their rich attire:
Blue, glossy green, and velvet black,
They coiled and swam; and every track
Was a flash of golden fire.

Their beauty and their
happiness.

O happy living things! no tongue
Their beauty might declare:
A spring of love gushed from my heart,
And I blessed them unaware:

He blesseth them in
his heart.

Sure my kind saint took pity on me,
And I blessed them unaware.

The self same moment I could pray;
And from my neck so free

The spell begins to
break.

The Albatross fell off, and sank
Like lead into the sea.

Beyond the shadow of the ship, / I watched the water-snakes:

PART THE FIFTH

OH sleep! it is a gentle thing,
Beloved from pole to pole!
To Mary Queen the praise be given!
She sent the gentle sleep from Heaven,
That slid into my soul.

By grace of the holy
Mother, the ancient
Mariner is refreshed
with rain.

The silly buckets on the deck,
That had so long remained,
I dreamt that they were filled with dew;
And when I awoke, it rained.

My lips were wet, my throat was cold,
My garments all were dank;
Sure I had drunken in my dreams,
And still my body drank.

I moved, and could not feel my limbs:
I was so light – almost
I thought that I had died in sleep,
And was a blesséd ghost.

He heareth sounds
and seeth strange
sights and
commotions in the sky
and the element.

And soon I heard a roaring wind:
It did not come anear;
But with its sound it shook the sails,
That were so thin and sere.

The upper air burst into life!
And a hundred fire-flags sheen,
To and fro they were hurried about!
And to and fro, and in and out,
The wan stars danced between.

And when I awoke, it rained.

And the coming wind did roar more loud,
And the sails did sigh like sedge;
And the rain poured down from one black cloud;
The Moon was at its edge.

The thick black cloud was cleft, and still
The Moon was at its side:
Like waters shot from some high crag,
The lightning fell with never a jag,
A river steep and wide.

The bodies of the
ship's crew are
inspired, and the ship
moves on;

The loud wind never reached the ship,
Yet now the ship moved on!
Beneath the lightning and the Moon
The dead men gave a groan.

They groaned, they stirred, they all uprose,
Nor spake, nor moved their eyes:
It had been strange, even in a dream,
To have seen those dead men rise.

The helmsman steered, the ship moved on;
Yet never a breeze up-blew!
The mariners all 'gan work the ropes,
Where they were wont to do:
They raised their limbs like lifeless tools –
We were a ghastly crew.

The body of my brother's son,
Stood by me, knee to knee:

But not by the souls of
the men, nor by
demons of earth or
middle air, but by a
blessed troop of
angelic spirits, sent
down by the invocation
of the guardian saint.

The body and I pulled at one rope,
But he said nought to me.

'I fear thee, ancient Mariner!'
Be calm, thou Wedding-Guest!
'Twas not those souls that fled in pain,
Which to their corses came again,
But a troop of spirits blest:

The body and I pulled at one rope, / But he said nought to me.

For when it dawned – they dropped their arms,
And clustered round the mast;
Sweet sounds rose slowly through their mouths,
And from their bodies passed.

Around, around, flew each sweet sound,
Then darted to the Sun;
Slowly the sounds came back again,
Now mixed, now one by one.

Sometimes a-dropping from the sky
I heard the sky-lark sing;
Sometimes all little birds that are,
How they seemed to fill the sea and air
With their sweet jargoning!

And now 'twas like all instruments,
Now like a lonely flute;
And now it is an angel's song,
That makes the Heavens be mute.

It ceased; yet still the sails made on
A pleasant noise till noon,
A noise like of a hidden brook
In the leafy month of June,
That to the sleeping woods all night
Singeth a quiet tune.

Till noon we quietly sailed on,
Yet never a breeze did breathe:
Slowly and smoothly went the ship,
Moved onward from beneath.

The lonesome Spirit from the South Pole carries on the ship as far as the Line, in obedience to the angelic troop, but still requireth vengeance.

Under the keel nine fathom deep,
From the land of mist and snow,
The spirit slid: and it was he
That made the ship to go.
The sails at noon left off their tune,
And the ship stood still also.

Around, around, flew each sweet sound, / Then darted to the Sun;

The Sun, right up above the mast,
Had fixed her to the ocean:
But in a minute she 'gan stir,
With a short uneasy motion –
Backwards and forwards half her length
With a short uneasy motion.

Then like a pawing horse let go,
She made a sudden bound:
It flung the blood into my head,
And I fell down in a swound.

The Polar Spirit's
fellow-demons, the
invisible inhabitants of
the element, take part
in his wrong; and two
of them relate, one to
the other, that
penance long and
heavy for the ancient
Mariner hath been
accorded to the Polar
Spirit, who returneth
southward.

How long in that same fit I lay,
I have not to declare;
But ere my living life returned,
I heard and in my soul discerned
Two VOICES in the air.

'Is it he?' quoth one, 'Is this the man?
By him who died on cross,
With his cruel bow he laid full low,
The harmless Albatross.

'The spirit who bideth by himself
In the land of mist and snow,
He loved the bird that loved the man
Who shot him with his bow.'

The other was a softer voice,
As soft as honey-dew:
Quoth he, 'The man hath penance done,
And penance more will do.'

It flung the blood into my head, / And I fell down in a swound.

PART THE SIXTH

FIRST VOICE.
BUT tell me, tell me! speak again,
Thy soft response renewing –
What makes that ship drive on so fast?
What is the ocean doing?

SECOND VOICE.
Still as a slave before his lord,
The ocean hath no blast;
His great bright eye most silently
Up to the Moon is cast –

If he may know which way to go;
For she guides him smooth or grim
See, brother, see! how graciously
She looketh down on him.

FIRST VOICE.
But why drives on that ship so fast,
Without or wave or wind?

SECOND VOICE.
The air is cut away before,
And closes from behind.

The Mariner hath been cast into a trance; for the angelic power causeth the vessel to drive northward faster than human life could endure.

See, brother, see! how graciously / She looketh down on him.

Fly, brother, fly! more high, more high!
Or we shall be belated:
For slow and slow that ship will go,
When the Mariner's trance is abated.

The supernatural
motion is retarded; the
Mariner awakes, and
his penance begins
anew.

I woke, and we were sailing on
As in a gentle weather:
'Twas night, calm night, the Moon was high;
The dead men stood together.

All stood together on the deck,
For a charnel-dungeon fitter:
All fixed on me their stony eyes,
That in the Moon did glitter.

The pang, the curse, with which they died,
Had never passed away:
I could not draw my eyes from theirs,
Nor turn them up to pray.

The curse if finally
expiated;

And now this spell was snapt: once more
I viewed the ocean green.
And looked far forth, yet little saw
Of what had else been seen –

Like one that on a lonesome road
Doth walk in fear and dread,
And having once turned round walks on,
And turns no more his head;
Because he knows a frightful fiend
Doth close behind him tread.

Fly, brother, fly! more high, more high! / Or we shall be belated:

But soon there breathed a wind on me,
Nor sound nor motion made:
Its path was not upon the sea,
In ripple or in shade.

It raised my hair, it fanned my cheek
Like a meadow-gale of spring –
It mingled strangely with my fears,
Yet it felt like a welcoming.

Swiftly, swiftly flew the ship,
Yet she sailed softly too:
Sweetly, sweetly blew the breeze –
On me alone it blew.

And the ancient
Mariner beholdeth his
native country.

Oh! dream of joy! is this indeed
The light-house top I see?
Is this the hill? is this the kirk?
Is this mine own countree?

We drifted o'er the harbour-bar,
And I with sobs did pray –
O let me be awake, my God!
Or let me sleep alway.

The harbour-bay was clear as glass,
So smoothly it was strewn!
And on the bay the moonlight lay,
And the shadow of the Moon.

Is this the hill? is this the kirk? / Is this mine own countree?

The rock shone bright, the kirk no less,
That stands above the rock:
The moonlight steeped in silentness
The steady weathercock.

And the bay was white with silent light,
Till rising from the same,
Full many shapes, that shadows were,
In crimson colours came.

The angelic spirits
leave the dead bodies,

A little distance from the prow
Those crimson shadows were:
I turned my eyes upon the deck –
Oh, Christ! what saw I there!

And appear in their
own forms of light.

Full many shapes, that shadows were, / In crimson colours came.

Each corse lay flat, lifeless and flat,
And, by the holy rood!
A man all light, a seraph-man,
On every corse there stood.

This seraph band, each waved his hand:
It was a heavenly sight!
They stood as signals to the land,
Each one a lovely light:

This seraph-band, each waved his hand,
No voice did they impart –
No voice; but oh! the silence sank
Like music on my heart.

But soon I heard the dash of oars;
I heard the Pilot's cheer;
My head was turned perforce away,
And I saw a boat appear.

The Pilot, and the Pilot's boy,
I heard them coming fast:
Dear Lord in Heaven! it was a joy
The dead men could not blast.

I saw a third – I heard his voice:
It is the Hermit good!
He singeth loud his godly hymns
That he makes in the wood.
He'll shrieve my soul, he'll wash away
The Albatross's blood.

A man all light, a seraph-man, / On every corse there stood.

PART THE SEVENTH

The Hermit of the
Wood,

THIS Hermit good lives in that wood
Which slopes down to the sea.
How loudly his sweet voice he rears!
He loves to talk with marineres
That come from a far countree.

He kneels at morn and noon and eve –
He hath a cushion plump:
It is the moss that wholly hides
The rotted old oak-stump.

The skiff-boat neared: I heard them talk,
'Why this is strange, I trow!
Where are those lights so many and fair,
That signal made but now?'

'Strange, by my faith!' the Hermit said –

Approacheth the ship
with wonder.

'And they answered not our cheer!
The planks looked warped! and see those sails,
How thin they are and sere!
I never saw aught like to them,
Unless perchance it were

'Brown skeletons of leaves that lag
My forest-brook along;
When the ivy-tod is heavy with snow,
And the owlet whoops to the wolf below,
That eats the she-wolf's young.'

The skiff-boat neared: I heard them talk, / 'Why this is strange, I trow!

'Dear Lord! it hath a fiendish look –
(The Pilot made reply)
I am a-feared–' 'Push on, push on!'
Said the Hermit cheerily.

The boat came closer to the ship,
But I nor spake nor stirred;
The boat came close beneath the ship,
And straight a sound was heard.

Under the water it rumbled on,
Still louder and more dread:
The ship suddenly
sinketh.
It reached the ship, it split the bay;
The ship went down like lead.

It reached the ship, it split the bay; / The ship went down like lead.

Stunned by that loud and dreadful sound,
Which sky and ocean smote,
Like one that hath been seven days drowned
My body lay afloat;
But swift as dreams, myself I found
Within the Pilot's boat.

The ancient Mariner is saved in the Pilot's boat.

Upon the whirl, where sank the ship,
The boat spun round and round;
And all was still, save that the hill
Was telling of the sound.

I moved my lips – the Pilot shrieked
And fell down in a fit;
The holy Hermit raised his eyes,
And prayed where he did sit.

I took the oars: the Pilot's boy,
Who now doth crazy go,
Laughed loud and long, and all the while
His eyes went to and fro.
'Ha! ha!' quoth he, 'full plain I see,
The Devil knows how to row.'

'Ha! ha!' quoth he, 'full plain I see, / The Devil knows how to row.'

And now, all in my own countree,
I stood on the firm land!
The Hermit stepped forth from the boat,
And scarcely he could stand.

The ancient Mariner
earnestly entreateth
the Hermit to shrieve
him; and the penance
of life falls on him.

'O shrieve me, shrieve me, holy man!'
The Hermit crossed his brow.
'Say quick,' quoth he, 'I bid thee say –
What manner of man art thou?'

Forthwith this frame of mine was wrenched
With a woeful agony,
Which forced me to begin my tale;
And then it left me free.

'Say quick,' quoth he, 'I bid thee say – / What manner of man art thou?'

And ever and anon
throughout his future
life an agony
constraineth him to
travel from land to
land,

Since then, at an uncertain hour,
That agony returns;
And till my ghastly tale is told,
This heart within me burns.

And till my ghastly tale is told, / This heart within me burns.

I pass, like night, from land to land;
I have strange power of speech;
That moment that his face I see,
I know the man that must hear me:
To him my tale I teach.

That moment that his face I see, / I know the man that must hear me:

What loud uproar bursts from that door!
The wedding-guests are there:
But in the garden-bower the bride
And bride-maids singing are:
And hark the little vesper bell,
Which biddeth me to prayer!

What loud uproar bursts from that door! / The wedding-guests are there:

O Wedding-Guest! this soul hath been
Alone on a wide wide sea:
So lonely 'twas, that God himself
Scarce seeméd there to be.

O sweeter than the marriage-feast,
'Tis sweeter far to me,
To walk together to the kirk
With a goodly company! –

To walk together to the kirk,
And all together pray,
While each to his great Father bends,
Old men, and babes, and loving friends,
And youths and maidens gay!

And to teach, by his
own example, love and
reverence to all things
that God made and
loveth.

Farewell, farewell! but this I tell
To thee, thou Wedding-Guest!
He prayeth well, who loveth well
Both man and bird and beast.

So lonely 'twas, that God himself / Scarce seeméd there to be.

He prayeth best, who loveth best
All things both great and small;
For the dear God who loveth us
He made and loveth all.

The Mariner, whose eye is bright,
Whose beard with age is hoar,
Is gone: and now the Wedding-Guest
Turned from the bridegroom's door.

He went like one that hath been stunned,
And is of sense forlorn:
A sadder and a wiser man,
He rose the morrow morn.

The Mariner, whose eye is bright, / Whose beard with age is hoar, / Is gone:

ASSORTED POEMS

KUBLA KHAN

In Xanadu did Kubla Khan
A stately pleasure-dome decree:
Where Alph, the sacred river, ran
Through caverns measureless to man
    Down to a sunless sea.
So twice five miles of fertile ground
With walls and towers were girdled round:
And there were gardens bright with sinuous rills
Where blossomed many an incense-bearing tree;
And here were forests ancient as the hills,
Enfolding sunny spots of greenery.

But oh ! that deep romantic chasm which slanted
Down the green hill athwart a cedarn cover!

A savage place ! as holy and enchanted
As e'er beneath a waning moon was haunted
By woman wailing for her demon-lover!
And from this chasm, with ceaseless turmoil seething,
As if this earth in fast thick pants were breathing,
A mighty fountain momently was forced:
Amid whose swift half-intermitted burst
Huge fragments vaulted like rebounding hail,
Or chaffy grain beneath the thresher's flail:
And mid these dancing rocks at once and ever
It flung up momently the sacred river.
Five miles meandering with a mazy motion
Through wood and dale the sacred river ran,
Then reached the caverns measureless to man,

And here were forests ancient as the hills, / Enfolding sunny spots of greenery.

And sank in tumult to a lifeless ocean:
And 'mid this tumult Kubla heard from far
Ancestral voices prophesying war!

    The shadow of the dome of pleasure
    Floated midway on the waves;
    Where was heard the mingled measure
    From the fountain and the caves.
It was a miracle of rare device,
A sunny pleasure-dome with caves of ice!
    A damsel with a dulcimer
    In a vision once I saw:
    It was an Abyssinian maid,
    And on her dulcimer she played,

    Singing of Mount Abora.
    Could I revive within me
    Her symphony and song,
    To such a deep delight 'twould win me,
That with music loud and long,
I would build that dome in air,
That sunny dome! those caves of ice!
And all who heard should see them there,
And all should cry, Beware! Beware!
His flashing eyes, his floating hair!
Weave a circle round him thrice,
And close your eyes with holy dread,
For he on honey-dew hath fed,
And drunk the milk of Paradise.

And sank in tumult to a lifeless ocean:

FROST AT MIDNIGHT

The Frost performs its secret ministry,
Unhelped by any wind. The owlet's cry
Came loud – and hark, again! loud as before.
The inmates of my cottage, all at rest,
Have left me to that solitude, which suits
Abstruser musings: save that at my side
My cradled infant slumbers peacefully.
'Tis calm indeed! so calm, that it disturbs
And vexes meditation with its strange
And extreme silentness. Sea, hill, and wood,
This populous village! Sea, and hill, and wood,
With all the numberless goings on of life,
Inaudible as dreams! the thin blue flame
Lies on my low burnt fire, and quivers not;

Only that film, which fluttered on the grate,
Still flutters there, the sole unquiet thing.
Methinks, its motion in this hush of nature
Gives it dim sympathies with me who live,
Making it a companionable form,
Whose puny flaps and freaks the idling Spirit
By its own moods interprets, every where
Echo or mirror seeking of itself,
And makes a toy of Thought.

     But O ! how oft,
How oft, at school, with most believing mind,
Presageful, have I gazed upon the bars,
To watch that fluttering stranger! and as oft

Sea, hill, and wood. / This populous village!

With unclosed lids, already had I dreamt
Of my sweet birth-place, and the old church-tower,
Whose bells, the poor man's only music, rang
From morn to evening, all the hot Fair-day,
So sweetly, that they stirred and haunted me
With a wild pleasure, falling on mine ear
Most like articulate sounds of things to come!
So gazed I, till the soothing things I dreamt,
Lulled me to sleep, and sleep prolonged my dreams!
And so I brooded all the following morn,
Awed by the stern preceptor's face, mine eye
Fixed with mock study on my swimming book :
Save if the door half opened, and I snatched
A hasty glance, and still my heart leaped up,

For still I hoped to see the stranger's face,
Townsman, or aunt, or sister more beloved,
My play-mate when we both were clothed alike!

Dear Babe, that sleepest cradled by my side,
Whose gentle breathings, heard in this deep calm,
Fill up the interspersed vacancies
And momentary pauses of the thought!
My babe so beautiful! it thrills my heart
With tender gladness, thus to look at thee,
And think that thou shalt learn far other lore
And in far other scenes! For I was reared
In the great city, pent 'mid cloisters dim,
And saw nought lovely but the sky and stars.

...the old church-tower, / Whose bells, the poor man's only music, rang

But thou, my babe! shalt wander like a breeze
By lakes and sandy shores, beneath the crags
Of ancient mountain, and beneath the clouds,
Which image in their bulk both lakes and shores
And mountain crags: so shalt thou see and hear
The lovely shapes and sounds intelligible
Of that eternal language, which thy God
Utters, who from eternity doth teach
Himself in all, and all things in himself.
Great universal Teacher! he shall mould
Thy spirit, and by giving make it ask.

Therefore all seasons shall be sweet to thee,
Whether the summer clothe the general earth
With greenness, or the redbreast sit and sing
Betwixt the tufts of snow on the bare branch
Of mossy apple-tree, while the nigh thatch
Smokes in the sun-thaw; whether the eve-drops fall
Heard only in the trances of the blast,
Or if the secret ministry of frost
Shall hang them up in silent icicles,
Quietly shining to the quiet Moon.

But thou, my babe! shalt wander like a breeze / By lakes and sandy shores

THIS LIME-TREE BOWER
MY PRISON

Well, they are gone, and here must I remain,
This lime-tree bower my prison! I have lost
Beauties and feelings, such as would have been
Most sweet to my remembrance even when age
Had dimmed mine eyes to blindness! They,
    meanwhile,
Friends, whom I never more may meet again,
On springy heath, along the hill-top edge,
Wander in gladness, and wind down, perchance,
To that still roaring dell, of which I told;
The roaring dell, o'erwooded, narrow, deep,
And only speckled by the mid-day sun;
Where its slim trunk the ash from rock to rock
Flings arching like a bridge; – that branchless ash,

Unsunned and damp, whose few poor yellow leaves
Ne'er tremble in the gale, yet tremble still,
Fanned by the water-fall! and there my friends
Behold the dark green file of long lank weeds,
That all at once (a most fantastic sight!)
Still nod and drip beneath the dripping edge
Of the blue clay-stone.

    Now, my friends emerge
Beneath the wide wide Heaven – and view again
The many-steepled tract magnificent
Of hilly fields and meadows, and the sea,
With some fair bark, perhaps, whose sails light up
The slip of smooth clear blue betwixt two Isles

The roaring dell, o'erwooded, narrow, deep,

Of purple shadow! Yes! they wander on
In gladness all; but thou, methinks, most glad,
My gentle-hearted Charles! for thou hast pined
And hungered after Nature, many a year,
In the great City pent, winning thy way
With sad yet patient soul, through evil and pain
And strange calamity! Ah! slowly sink
Behind the western ridge, thou glorious Sun!
Shine in the slant beams of the sinking orb,
Ye purple heath-flowers! richlier burn, ye clouds!
Live in the yellow light, ye distant groves!
And kindle, thou blue Ocean! So my Friend
Struck with deep joy may stand, as I have stood,
Silent with swimming sense; yea, gazing round

On the wide landscape, gaze till all doth seem
Less gross than bodily; and of such hues
As veil the Almighty Spirit, when yet he makes
Spirits perceive his presence.

   A delight
Comes sudden on my heart, and I am glad
As I myself were there! Nor in this bower,
This little lime-tree bower, have I not marked
Much that has sooth'd me. Pale beneath the blaze
Hung the transparent foliage; and I watched
Some broad and sunny leaf, and loved to see
The shadow of the leaf and stem above
Dappling its sunshine! And that walnut-tree

...for thou hast pined / And hungered after Nature, many a year, / In the great City pent

Was richly tinged, and a deep radiance lay
Full on the ancient ivy, which usurps
Those fronting elms, and now, with blackest mass
Makes their dark branches gleam a lighter hue
Through the late twilight: and though now the bat
Wheels silent by, and not a swallow twitters,
Yet still the solitary humble bee
Sings in the bean-flower ! Henceforth I shall know
That Nature ne'er deserts the wise and pure;
No plot so narrow, be but Nature there,
No waste so vacant, but may well employ
Each faculty of sense, and keep the heart
Awake to Love and Beauty! and sometimes
'Tis well to be bereft of promised good,

That we may lift the Soul, and contemplate
With lively joy the joys we cannot share.
My gentle-hearted Charles! when the last rook
Beat its straight path across the dusky air
Homewards, I blest it! deeming, its black wing
(Now a dim speck, now vanishing in light)
Had crossed the mighty orb's dilated glory,
While thou stood'st gazing; or when all was still,
Flew creeking o'er thy head, and had a charm
For thee, my gentle-hearted Charles, to whom
No sound is dissonant which tells of Life.

...Nature ne'er deserts the wise and pure; / No plot so narrow, be but Nature there,

DEJECTION: AN ODE

Late, late yestreen I saw the new Moon,
With the old Moon in her arms;
And I fear, I fear, My Master dear!
We shall have a deadly storm.

BALLAD OF SIR PATRICK SPENCE.

I
WELL! If the Bard was weather-wise, who made
    The grand old ballad of Sir Patrick Spence,
    This night, so tranquil now, will not go hence
Unroused by winds, that ply a busier trade
Than those which mould yon cloud in lazy flakes,
Or the dull sobbing draft, that moans and rakes
    Upon the strings of this Eolian lute,
    Which better far were mute.
For lo! the New-moon winter-bright!
And overspread with phantom light,
    (With swimming phantom light o'erspread
    But rimmed and circled by a silver thread)
I see the old Moon in her lap, foretelling
    The coming-on of rain and squally blast.
And oh ! that even now the gust were swelling,
    And the slant night-shower driving loud and fast!
Those sounds which oft have raised me, whilst they awed,
    And sent my soul abroad,
Might now perhaps their wonted impulse give,
Might startle this dull pain, and make it move and live!

...the old Moon in her lap, foretelling / The coming-on of rain and squally blast.

II

A grief without a pang, void, dark, and drear,
    A stifled, drowsy, unimpassioned grief,
    Which finds no natural outlet, no relief,
    In word, or sigh, or tear –
O Lady! in this wan and heartless mood,
To other thoughts by yonder throstle woo'd,
    All this long eve, so balmy and serene,
Have I been gazing on the western sky,
    And its peculiar tint of yellow green:
And still I gaze – and with how blank an eye!
And those thin clouds above, in flakes and bars,
That give away their motion to the stars;
Those stars, that glide behind them or between,

Now sparkling, now bedimmed, but always seen:
Yon crescent Moon, as fixed as if it grew
In its own cloudless, starless lake of blue;
I see them all so excellently fair,
I see, not feel, how beautiful they are!

III

    My genial spirits fail;
    And what can these avail
To lift the smothering weight from off my breast?
    It were a vain endeavour,
    Though I should gaze for ever
On that green light that lingers in the west:
I may not hope from outward forms to win

Yon crescent Moon, as fixed as if it grew / In its own cloudless, starless lake of blue;

The passion and the life, whose fountains are
    within.

IV
O Lady! we receive but what we give,
And in our life alone does nature live:
Ours is her wedding-garment, ours her shroud!
    And would we aught behold, of higher worth,
Than that inanimate cold world allowed
To the poor loveless ever-anxious crowd,
    Ah! from the soul itself must issue forth,
A light, a glory, a fair luminous cloud
    Enveloping the Earth –
And from the soul itself must there be sent

A sweet and potent voice, of its own birth,
Of all sweet sounds the life and element!

V
O pure of heart! thou need'st not ask of me
What this strong music in the soul may be!
What, and wherein it doth exist,
This light, this glory, this fair luminous mist,
This beautiful and beauty-making power.
    Joy, virtuous Lady! Joy that ne'er was given,
Save to the pure, and in their purest hour,
Life, and Life's effluence, cloud at once and shower,
Joy, Lady! is the spirit and the power,
Which wedding Nature to us gives in dower

Joy, Lady! is the spirit and the power, / Which wedding Nature to us gives in dower

A new Earth and new Heaven,
Undreamt of by the sensual and the proud –
Joy is the sweet voice, Joy the luminous cloud –
    We in ourselves rejoice!
And thence flows all that charms or ear or sight,
    All melodies the echoes of that voice,
All colours a suffusion from that light.

VI
There was a time when, though my path was rough,
    This joy within me dallied with distress,
And all misfortunes were but as the stuff
    Whence Fancy made me dreams of happiness:
For hope grew round me, like the twining vine,

And fruits, and foliage, not my own, seemed mine.
But now afflictions bow me down to earth:
Nor care I that they rob me of my mirth,
    But oh! each visitation
Suspends what nature gave me at my birth,
    My shaping spirit of Imagination.
For not to think of what I needs must feel,
    But to be still and patient, all I can;
And haply by abstruse research to steal
    From my own nature all the natural man –
    This was my sole resource, my only plan:
Till that which suits a part infects the whole,
And now is almost grown the habit of my soul.

And fruits, and foliage, not my own, seemed mine.

VII

Hence, viper thoughts, that coil around my mind,
    Reality's dark dream!
I turn from you, and listen to the wind,
    Which long has raved unnoticed. What a
    scream
Of agony by torture lengthened out
That lute sent forth! Thou Wind, that rav'st
    without,
    Bare crag, or mountain-tairn, or blasted tree,
Or pine-grove whither woodman never clomb,
Or lonely house, long held the witches' home,
    Methinks were fitter instruments for thee,
Mad Lutanist! who in this month of showers,

Of dark brown gardens, and of peeping flowers,
Mak'st Devils' yule, with worse than wintry song,
The blossoms, buds, and timorous leaves among.
    Thou Actor, perfect in all tragic sounds!
Thou mighty Poet, e'en to frenzy bold!
    What tell'st thou now about?
    'Tis of the rushing of a host in rout,
With groans, of trampled men, with smarting
    wounds –
At once they groan with pain, and shudder with the cold!
But hush! there is a pause of deepest silence!
    And all that noise, as of a rushing crowd,
With groans, and tremulous shudderings – all is over –
    It tells another tale, with sounds less deep and loud!

Thou Wind, that rav'st without, / Bare crag, or mountain-tairn, or blasted tree,

A tale of less affright,
  And tempered with delight,
As Otway's self had framed the tender lay,
    'Tis of a little child
    Upon a lonesome wild,
Not far from home, but she hath lost her way:
And now moans low in bitter grief and fear,
And now screams loud, and hopes to make her
    mother hear.

VIII

'Tis midnight, but small thoughts have I of sleep:
Full seldom may my friend such vigils keep!
Visit her, gentle Sleep! with wings of healing,
    And may this storm be but a mountain-birth,
May all the stars hang bright above her dwelling,
    Silent as though they watch'd the sleeping
    Earth!
    With light heart may she rise,
    Gay fancy, cheerful eyes,
    Joy lift her spirit, joy attune her voice:
To her may all things live, from pole to pole,
Their life the eddying of her living soul!
    O simple spirit, guided from above,
Dear Lady! friend devoutest of my choice,
Thus may'st thou ever, evermore rejoice.

May all the stars hang bright above her dwelling, / Silent as though they watch'd the sleeping Earth!

YOUTH AND AGE

Verse, a Breeze mid blossoms straying,
Where Hope clung feeding, like a bee –
Both were mine! Life went a maying
    With Nature, Hope, and Poesy,
    When I was young!
When I was young? – Ah, woful When!
Ah! for the change 'twixt Now and Then!
This breathing house not built with hands,
This body that does me grievous wrong,
O'er aery cliffs and glittering sands,
How lightly then it flashed along: –
Like those trim skiffs, unknown of yore,
On winding lakes and rivers wide,
That ask no aid of sail or oar,

That fear no spite of wind or tide!
Nought cared this body for wind or weather
When Youth and I lived in't together.

Flowers are lovely; Love is flower-like;
Friendship is a sheltering tree;
O! the joys, that came down shower-like,
Of Friendship, Love, and Liberty,
    Ere I was old!
Ere I was old? Ah woful Ere,
Which tells me, Youth's no longer here!
O Youth! for years so many and sweet,
'Tis known, that Thou and I were one,
I'll think it but a fond conceit –

Flowers are lovely; Love is flower-like; / Friendship is a sheltering tree;

It cannot be, that Thou art gone!
Thy vesper-bell hath not yet toll'd: –
And thou wert aye a masker bold!
What strange disguise hast now put on,
To make believe, that Thou art gone?
I see these locks in silvery slips,
This drooping gait, this altered size:
But springtide blossoms on thy lips,
And tears take sunshine from thine eyes!
Life is but thought: so think I will
That Youth and I are house-mates still.

Dew-drops are the gems of morning,
But the tears of mournful eve!

Where no hope is, life's a warning
That only serves to make us grieve,
     When we are old:
That only serves to make us grieve
With oft and tedious taking-leave,
Like some poor nigh-related guest,
That may not rudely be dismist:
Yet hath outstay'd his welcome while,
And tells the jest without the smile.

It cannot be, that Thou art gone! / Thy vesper-bell hath not yet toll'd: –

WORK WITHOUT HOPE

ALL Nature seems at work. Slugs leave their lair –
The bees are stirring – birds are on the wing –
And Winter slumbering in the open air,
Wears on his smiling face a dream of Spring!
And I, the while, the sole unbusy thing,
Nor honey make, nor pair, nor build, nor sing.

Yet well I ken the banks where amaranths blow,
Have traced the fount whence streams of nectar flow.

Bloom, O ye Amaranths! bloom for whom ye may,
For me ye bloom not! Glide, rich streams, away!
With lips unbrightened, wreathless brow, I stroll:
And would you learn the spells that drowse my
    soul?
Work without hope draws nectar in a sieve,
And Hope without an object cannot live.

Yet well I ken the banks where aramanths blow,

EPITAPH

Stop, Christian Passer-by: Stop, child of God,
And read, with gentle breast. Beneath this sod
A poet lies, or that which once seem'd he –
O, lift one thought in prayer for S. T. C.;
That he who many a year with toil of breath
Found death in life, may here find life in death!
Mercy for praise – to be forgiven for fame
He ask'd, and hoped, through Christ. Do thou
the same!

Stop, child of God, / And read, with gentle breast. Beneath this sod / A poet lies,

ACKNOWLEDGEMENTS

Images on pages 1–93 are reproduced with the permission of Dover Publications from their edition: *The Rime of the Ancient Mariner*

Images on pages 94-99, 101, 108 and 111 are reproduced with the permission of Dover Publications from their edition: *1800 Woodcuts by Thomas Bewick and his School*

Images on pages 100, 102-107 and 109-110 are from Clipart

Dates of versions of Additional Poems:

Kubla Khan: Autumn of 1797 or (more likely) spring of 1798, published 1816, 1828, 1829, 1834
(proofed against E. H. Coleridge's 1927 edition of STC's poems and a *c.* 1898 edition of STC's Poetical Works, "reprinted from the early editions")

Frost at Midnight: February 1798, published 1798, 1808, 1812, 1817, 1828, 1829, 1834
(proofed against E. H. Coleridge's 1927 edition of STC's poems and a *c.* 1898 edition of STC's Poetical Works, "reprinted from the early editions")

This Lime-Tree Bower My Prison: 1797, published 1800, 1810, 1817, 1828, 1829, 1834
(proofed against E. H. Coleridge's 1927 edition of STC's poems and a *c.* 1898 edition of STC's Poetical Works, "reprinted from the early editions")

Dejection: An Ode: 1802, published 1802, 1817, 1828, 1829, 1834
(proofed against E. H. Coleridge's 1927 edition of STC's poems and a *c.* 1898 edition of STC's Poetical Works, "reprinted from the early editions")

Youth and Age: 1823-1832, published 1834; lines 1-38 were published as Youth and Age 1828, 1829, and lines 39-49 as An Old Man's Sigh in 1832
(proofed against E. H. Coleridge's 1927 edition of STC's poems and a *c.* 1898 edition of STC's Poetical Works, "reprinted from the early editions")

Work without Hope: 1825, published 1828, 1829, 1834
(proofed against E. H. Coleridge's 1927 edition of STC's poems and a *c.* 1898 edition of STC's Poetical Works, "reprinted from the early editions")

Epitaph: November 9, 1833, published 1834
(proofed against E. H. Coleridge's 1927 edition of STC's poems and a *c.* 1898 edition of STC's Poetical Works, "reprinted from the early editions")